SCUBA DIVING
... to the Extreme:

Off the Wall

YOUTH FICTION
BY SIGMUND BROUWER

Short Cuts Series
#1 *Snowboarding . . . to the Extreme: Rippin'*
#2 *Mountain Biking . . . to the Extreme: Cliff Dive*
#3 *Skydiving . . . to the Extreme: 'Chute Roll*
#4 *Scuba Diving . . . to the Extreme: Off the Wall*

Lightning on Ice Series
#1 *Rebel Glory*
#2 *All-Star Pride*
#3 *Thunderbird Spirit*
#4 *Winter Hawk Star*
#5 *Blazer Drive*
#6 *Chief Honor*

The Accidental Detectives Mystery Series

Winds of Light Medieval Adventures

SCUBA DIVING
... to the Extreme:

Off the Wall

Sigmund Brouwer

WORD PUBLISHING

Dallas·London·Vancouver·Melbourne

Scuba Diving . . . to the Extreme: Off the Wall

Managing Editor: Laura Minchew
Project Editor: Beverly Phillips

Library of Congress Cataloging-in-Publication Data

Brouwer, Sigmund, 1959–
   Scuba diving—to the extreme—off the wall /
   Sigmund Brouwer.
      p. cm. — (Short cuts ; 4)
   "Word kids!"
   Summary: While helping his uncle run a scuba
diving shop, Ian becomes involved in a diving mishap
that proves to be no accident.
   ISBN 0-8499-3954-2 (trade paper)
   [1. Buried treasure—Fiction. 2. Scuba diving—
Fiction. 3. Mystery and detective stories.] I. Title.
II. Series: Brouwer, Sigmund, 1959–   Short cuts ; 4.
PZ7.B79984Sc   1997
[Fic]—dc21

                                          96-44834
                                             CIP
                                              AC

Printed in the United States of America

98 99 00 OPM 9 8 7 6 5 4 3 2

To
Kate and Grant—
Someday I hope you'll understand
how much vision, spirit, and soul your
mother has added to the world of
childrens' book publishing.

Chapter One

Think of a ten-story building. In your mind, tip it upside down. Now picture how far the top of the building would reach under water. That's about 100 feet down. That's where I was headed at 10:00 on a hot Thursday morning in August. Diving to a shipwreck, 100 feet straight down.

I was three miles off shore in the warm ocean near Key Largo in Florida. I had already swum 20 feet down. There was a thin nylon line on my weight belt. It was snapped to a cable that dropped from the boat above. On the other end of the cable was a heavy anchor. Being hooked to this line made it easy for me to go straight down in the Gulf current.

Normally, I wouldn't use a guideline. I'd take my time and let the current just take me. But this was a work dive, not a fun dive. Normally, I would have a partner. Diving alone is not smart. But my Uncle Gord couldn't afford to hire another diver. So just this once, I was alone. Besides, all I had to do was go down, then up. Simple and safe.

At 30 feet deep, I tilted my head to look up at the surface. The shadow of the *GypSea*—my uncle's dive boat—was a long black shape. It looked like a fat cigar floating above me.

Far below me was another boat. This one was much larger than the *GypSea*. And it was in pretty bad shape. The shipwreck was called the *Duane*. It was an old Coast Guard ship. There was no cool story about it sinking in a storm or anything like that. The *Duane* had been cleaned up and then sunk on purpose. It was sunk to make a reef, a nice hiding place for fish and other undersea animals. It was also sunk so tourists could scuba dive and explore it.

Tourists were part of my job. In fact, I was diving down to the wreck so I could hide a toy treasure chest for them. It was my idea. Business had not been good for a while. More people might hire my uncle's boat for dives if we set up a treasure hunt for them.

The toy treasure chest I carried was not much bigger than a football. Inside it was a hundred-dollar bill sealed in a plastic bag to keep it dry. We were hiding it deep for experienced divers.

I kicked my fins and swam down another ten feet. Slowly.

I don't like to hurry when I scuba dive. I also check and double-check everything. All the time. There is a saying in this sport: *There are old divers and there are bold divers, but there are no old, bold divers.* In other words, mistakes can kill you.

I dropped another 10 feet. I was down to 50 feet. I stopped and hit a button to pump some air from my tank into special pockets built into my vest. I did this because, as you go deeper, the weight of the water makes it harder to swim. By adding air to my vest, I was able to make myself lighter.

3

As I swam, I turned my head and watched for sharks. Especially hammerheads. Around Key Largo, they can be as long as a car. But much more dangerous. Cars just need gasoline for fuel. Sharks need meat and blood. I didn't want to be a quick fill up for a shark.

I didn't see any sharks. I saw plenty of smaller fish. Although I knew they were very colorful, they looked bluish gray. Even clear water soaks up colors. After 50 feet, reds and oranges and yellows are gone. The blue colors go after 60 feet.

At 65 feet deep, I checked the dial on my air tank. Solo diving needed extra care. Above me, in the *GypSea*, a guy named Judd Warner was waiting for me. He had just been hired by my uncle. Judd expected me back in a half hour.

At 70 feet deep in the water, I swallowed hard and popped my ears, something I had been doing all the way down. I did this to keep my eardrums from exploding.

At 75 feet, the ship below me was as big as a football field. I was only a few minutes away from it. It seemed ghostly in the dim water.

I finally reached the shipwreck at 100 feet. I found a place to hide the treasure chest and began to rise again.

It happened fifteen minutes later on my way up. At 53 feet deep, something ripped my mouthpiece away from my face. And the water around me exploded.

Chapter Two

I **was still attached** to the cable that was my guideline. For a couple of seconds, I bucked and danced at the end of my line. I felt like a rag doll shaken by a giant. Air bubbles kept exploding around my face mask. I grabbed my backup mouthpiece. It didn't work!

I tried to grab the main mouthpiece. At least it had air. The rubber tube was like a live snake. It twisted and turned in the water, trying to get away from me.

The air bubbles were coming from the mouthpiece. Air is squeezed into tanks under great pressure—3,000 pounds per square inch. A valve lets the air out slowly when you breathe. But the valve must have broken. The pressure was escaping, all at once. It was escaping through my mouth-piece. In a hurry. I was losing so much air and losing it so fast that the force of it was shaking my entire body.

I finally got my hands around the mouth-piece tube. I pulled the mouthpiece toward me. But there was no way I could put it back into my mouth. The air was shooting out too hard. Trying to breathe air from it would have been like trying to sip water from a fire hose.

But I needed air. Badly. And soon. I was 53 feet under water.

Chapter Three

I tried to stay calm. In scuba diving, if you stop thinking, you're in trouble.

I knew I had two problems. One problem, of course, was I needed air. There was lots of it above the water. But I'd have to swim 53 feet straight up to get to it.

Except it wouldn't be that easy. And that was my other problem. If I didn't do it right, my lungs would explode. There was a simple reason for this. The deeper you go, the more the weight of the water squeezes things. Including air.

Once, my Uncle Gord showed me exactly

how it worked. He took me 33 feet under water. We also took an empty plastic milk jug. He held the jug upside down and filled it with air from his scuba tank. He put the cap on the jug. He held onto the jug by a piece of a rope tied around its handle. The jug floated up, like a balloon on a string.

I followed him as we swam deeper and deeper. The pressure of the water squeezed the jug. It looked like an invisible hand was crushing it. At 66 feet deep, the jug was half the size it had been.

This works the same in reverse. As you rise, there is less weight and the water squeezes less. The same amount of air takes up more space.

At 66 feet deep Uncle Gord had added air to the crushed jug from his scuba tank. He filled it until it was normal size again and put the cap back on. Then we swam up, following the jug as it got closer and closer to the surface. As we got higher, the air in the jug pushed out because there was less water pressure squeezing it. It was like watching someone blow up a balloon. At 33 feet, the air inside expanded so much that the plastic jug ripped wide open.

That's what would happen to my lungs if I swam up too quickly. Fifty feet higher, the air now inside my lungs would take up double the space. My lungs would explode.

Or if they just ripped a little, air bubbles would get into my blood. This doesn't sound as bad as exploding lungs, but once those bubbles reached my brain, I'd be dead.

Fifty-three feet from the top, and running out of air, I thought of all of this.

There was only one thing to do.

I unsnapped myself from the guideline. I dropped my weight belt and kicked upward. Already I wanted to suck for air. But I forced myself to breathe out instead. My only chance was to keep pushing air out of my lungs. I didn't want them to explode like the plastic milk jug had.

I kicked more. I kept pushing air out of my lungs. My body screamed at me. It wanted all the air it could get. But if I held my breath, my lungs would rip.

Higher and higher. Second after second. I kept breathing out, kept pushing air out of my starving lungs.

Just like a cork, I began moving faster and

faster. There was still air in my diving vest. I had pumped it in on my way down. That air was taking me higher and faster.

I felt something punch at my chest. It was an air pocket in the vest. It blew apart as the air inside it expanded. It reminded me to keep pushing air out of my lungs, no matter what.

My sight became fuzzy and black around the edges. I needed air so badly I was about to pass out. But if I did, my body would try to breathe. My lungs would suck in water, not air.

The water grew brighter and brighter. Would I make it to the surface in time?

Then I remembered.

The boat!

If I was going straight up, I would hit the boat. Like a cork popping out of water. But corks don't have skulls that can be smashed. I did.

With my last energy, I kicked with my legs, trying to move sideways as I rose. I kicked. Kicked. Kicked . . .

The black around the edges of my eyesight filled in more and more. I heard roaring in my ears. And finally, I hit sweet air.

My body popped all the way out of the water. When I splashed back down, I saw the outline of the boat. Only ten feet away.

I sucked in lungful after lungful of air. Nothing in my life had felt better.

It had been close. Too close.

I waited for some energy to return. I swam toward the boat.

Judd leaned over. His face showed worry.

"Ian? Ian? What's the matter?"

I waved at him. It was a weak wave. I didn't have the strength for anything else. Not even the strength to talk.

I bumped up against the ladder. I tried to climb, but I couldn't. Judd reached down and helped me out of the water.

I got onto the boat.

"What happened?" Judd asked.

I groaned.

Water drained from my wet suit and my gear. I unbuckled my tank and vest and let both fall to the deck of the boat. I limped toward a bench. I let myself down. I lay back, staring up at the blue sky and waited.

There was still a chance I would die.

Chapter Four

Divers call it "the bends." They call it that because when you get it, you are forced to bend over with pain. It is a horrible pain. It hits the joints of elbows and legs. If it's bad enough, it can make you blind or kill you.

I wondered if the bends would hit me.

As I waited, I closed my eyes against the hot Florida sun. Seagulls, thinking we were a fishing boat, screamed as they flew in circles above.

"Ian?" Judd said. "Talk to me, man."

"I'm scared I came up too fast." My throat was sore from sucking in air.

"What!" His voice told me he knew my fear. "But why?"

He didn't say the rest. He didn't say that only a stupid diver would come up fast.

"I think the valve went on my tank. My tank was blowing air. I had nothing to breathe. Not even my backup."

"You made an emergency rise?"

"Yup." I groaned again. "No choice."

"How fast?"

"It happened at 53 feet. I came up on one last lungful of air."

"Straight up? Full speed?"

"You saw me pop out of the water."

"That's not good," he said. "How do you feel?"

"I don't know." I tried to smile. "Yet."

He stepped past me and started the boat engines. Judd Warner was big. At six feet one, he had an inch of height on me and about twenty pounds. I'm seventeen. I guessed him to be about ten years older. His hair was bleached blond by the sun and stringy from hours in saltwater. He wore shorts and a loose tank top and moved with the smooth lightness of a cat.

"We're heading in," he said. "We've got to get you to a chamber."

I wasn't going to argue. He wanted to get me in a pressure chamber at the hospital. The best way to fight the bends was to keep it from happening.

Uncle Gord had explained the bends to me by telling me to think of a bottle of cola. Shake it hard and quickly unscrew the lid. Watch it bubble over. Then think of bubbles popping out of your blood in the same way. Major pain.

It has to do with the same water pressure that squeezed Uncle Gord's milk jug.

The normal air that you breathe every day has nitrogen in it, along with oxygen. Scuba diving tanks have the same mixture. As you breathe under water, the pressure of the water slowly forces the nitrogen gas into your blood. The longer you stay, the more nitrogen in your blood.

It's not a problem, as long as you make sure the nitrogen gas leaves just as slowly as it went in. Just like with a bottle of cola. If you unscrew the lid a little at a time, the pressure is released slowly. The pop doesn't fizz.

But if you go up too fast in diving, you take the pressure off too fast. You become like a bottle of cola with the lid popped off. The pressure lets go all at once, and the gases inside the cola make bubbles and fizz over. Except in diving, the bubbles fizz in your blood. That's bad news.

It was the same bad news for me. Instead of going up at the ideal rate of 15 feet per minute, I had shot upward like a cork. I had been down so long there was a fifty-fifty chance that nitrogen bubbles were already getting ready to form in my blood.

Judd had both boat motors at full speed. We bounced across the green-blue water at 40 knots.

If I was going to get the bends, my only hope was to get to a hospital as fast as possible. The doctors would put me in a body-sized tube, close both ends, and pump a lot of air into it. That's a pressure chamber. Adding pressure would be like putting a lid back on the bottle of cola to stop the fizzing.

I tried not to think about what could happen if we didn't get there in time.

"I'm sorry man!" Judd shouted as we cut across open water. The wind blew his hair straight back. "It should have been me down there!"

"That's okay," I said. "Remember? It was my idea."

I don't think he heard me. I was too weak to shout above the wind.

As we got closer to shore, I wondered if Judd was thinking what I was thinking. Things like broken valves don't often happen to scuba diving tanks by accident.

That left two questions. Who had wrecked the valve? And why?

Chapter Five

Six hours later, I was in the back room of Uncle Gord's dive shop. Not dead. Not blind. Not bending over in pain. I had spent four hours in the chamber, and the doctor had sent me on my way.

"Your guess was right, Ian," he said. "The broken valve wasn't an accident."

Uncle Gord was my mother's brother. I lived in Miami during the school year. But for four summers now, I'd come down here to Key Largo to help Uncle Gord. He was a bit moody and liked to keep to himself. But we got along okay. The work wasn't bad.

The pay wasn't bad. And it never hurts to have your uncle as a boss.

"Look at this," he said.

He was standing at a workbench. Tools were scattered across the top of it. The valve parts of my scuba tank were in front of him.

I moved beside him to look.

Like my mother, Uncle Gord has hair that turned gray early. He has a bushy mustache that is still as dark as the rest of his hair used to be. Like my mother, he's not real big. But he's in great shape from diving all the time. He's in his forties, but I doubt many people would want to mess with him in a fight.

"See," he said, pointing. "Look at where the spring broke apart."

The spring was from the valve. It was strong enough to keep the valve partly closed against the air pressure inside the tank. Except it had broken in two pieces.

"Yes?" I wasn't sure what he meant.

"Take the magnifying glass."

I did. As I looked at it real close, he kept talking.

"It's like a tree you cut with a saw," he said. Uncle Gord loved using examples. "The cut is smooth most of the way through.

But when the tree falls, the last little bit breaks away and isn't smooth."

He was right. One side of the broken spring was shiny, as if it had been snipped halfway through. The other side was jagged, like it had been ripped apart.

"I don't get it," I said.

"I do," he told me. He frowned. "And I don't like it."

I waited.

"You know all about water pressure," he said.

I nodded yes. It had just about killed me a few hours earlier.

"Someone took this valve apart and cut most of the way through the spring. Then he put it back together. The spring was still strong enough to hold in shallow water. But in deeper water, it would only be a matter of time before the pressure blew it apart."

"In other words," I said, "someone wanted this accident to happen in deep water."

"Exactly. Whoever did this also plugged the backup mouthpiece. Someone wanted a serious accident to happen. What if you were inside the shipwreck when this happened?"

I gulped. Sometimes it takes a while just to swim out of a wreck.

"I'd be dead," I told him.

Uncle Gord stared at me for nearly a minute. He has light blue eyes. They didn't blink as he thought.

"I already know a lot of the story," he finally said. "You dove instead of Judd."

"Yes sir," I said.

"Even though I told you I wanted you on the surface."

"I've dived lots," I said. "You taught me to be careful. I didn't think you'd mind."

"What I mind is that Judd didn't do what I paid him to."

"Yes sir."

Uncle Gord stared at me for another minute. I remembered stories I'd heard about him getting into fights when he was younger. I'd heard he was tougher than most guys twice his size. By the cold look in his eyes, I could believe it.

"Tell me," he said. "Did you ask Judd if you could make the dive? Or did he ask you?"

My body suddenly felt as cold as Uncle Gord's eyes. I understood his question. If

Judd had asked me to go down, maybe he knew about the valve, that it would bust in deep water.

"I asked to dive," I said. "Honest. It was my idea. I was bored and wanted something to do. It was my fault this happened."

Uncle Gord slammed the workbench so hard that a wrench jumped and fell to the floor.

"It wasn't your fault," he said, his face angry. "It was whoever cut the valve spring."

He hit the table again. "I'm going to find out who did this."

Uncle Gord took a deep breath. He waited until he was calm.

"Ian," he said. "You and I are going to keep this a secret. That way, whoever did it won't know we're looking for him."

"What about the police?" I asked. "Shouldn't they know?"

Uncle Gord put his hands on my shoulders. He looked right into my eyes. "You know that business has not been great this year. What's going to happen if people hear about this? They'll think we don't run safe dives. They might not buy equipment from us."

"But—"

"No buts. I think I know why this happened," he said. "I'm going to tell you another secret: the real reason why I take the dive boat out on Friday and Saturday nights."

I had made my own guesses about why the valve might have been broken.

I asked Uncle Gord a simple question. "Does this have anything to do with a sunken pirate ship and a ton of gold?"

Chapter Six

Uncle Gord's square jaw fell. For a second, with his eyes bugged out and his mouth open wide, he looked like a fish just pulled from the water.

"How did you know about that!" he said.

"I don't think it's much of a secret," I said. "This is a small town."

"Tell me what you know. Tell me how you know," he quietly demanded.

I shrugged. "I heard the rumor two weeks ago. When I was with Judd. We were at the dock, putting gas in the dive boat. One of the guys there asked me if it was true that you were looking for a pirate ship."

"And?" Uncle Gord seemed worried.

"I told the guy I didn't know. Which was true. But I've been wondering. Along with a lot of other people in town. Everyone knows you go out every week with those three lawyers from Miami. No one believes that you are just spearfishing."

Three men had hired Uncle Gord every weekend since the beginning of May. Each Friday and Saturday night, Uncle Gord left at sunset with them and didn't return until dawn.

"Spearfishing is what we've wanted people to believe," Uncle Gord finally said. "But once you heard the rumors, why didn't you ask me about it?"

"It isn't my business," I said. "I figured you'd tell me if you ever wanted me to know."

Uncle Gord let out a deep breath. "I was afraid of this. That's why I don't like what happened to the valve on your scuba tank. If our secret is out, maybe someone wants to stop us."

"Will you tell me about it now?" I asked. "Is it really true what people are saying?"

"Let's walk down to the coffee shop. Nobody will be around this time of day. I'll tell you what I can."

Chapter Seven

Thelma's Diner was just down the road from Uncle Gord's dive shop. It was late afternoon and the sun was still strong and hot. When we got inside, Thelma came over to our table.

"What will it be, boys?" She was tall with brown hair. She had five kids and ran the diner by herself. She always looked tired.

"Same as always," Uncle Gord said. "A couple of iced teas. A couple orders of fries."

"Sure." She wiped our table. A minute later she brought the iced tea. Then she went into the kitchen. There was no one else in the diner. Uncle Gord and I could talk and not worry that someone would hear.

"I'm waiting," I said.

Uncle Gord drank half of his tea before he spoke. "I'll make the story as short as I can. It started in the spring when three lawyers came down here from Miami. They told me the story."

I added sugar to my iced tea and stirred as I listened.

"Some guy was scuba diving a couple miles from here. He found some gold coins about 30 feet deep. They looked very old and valuable. He hired the law firm to find out more about the coins."

"Why a law firm?" I asked.

"He made the lawyers sign an agreement to keep it secret. He knew if they didn't, he could sue them. He also wanted them to help him keep the rest of the treasure once he found it."

"It doesn't seem like the lawyers kept it much of a secret," I said.

"You're right. But the guy died just after he hired them. He didn't have a family or anything. Once he died, the lawyers figured they might as well look for the treasure themselves."

"Treasure," I said. "Real treasure. Not like the toy treasure I hid in the shipwreck for you this morning."

"Real treasure. Big, big treasure. The lawyers found out more about the coins. . . ."

Uncle Gord leaned forward across the table. His voice became a whisper. "Ian, they had a professor look at the coins. They're from a Spanish ship that sailed in the 1700s. It was delivering gold from the King of Spain. Pirates hit the ship and took everything. A week later, the pirate ship went down in a hurricane off the coast of Florida. The coins today would be worth more than ten million dollars."

It took me a second to realize I was sucking air through my straw. I was listening so close, I had drunk all my iced tea without knowing it.

"You know this for sure?" I asked.

"For sure," he said. "The lawyers did careful research in libraries and museums. These coins were made for a special occasion: the birth of the king's daughter. They could have only come from one ship."

"But what about the guy who found the coins? Didn't he find the ship too?"

"Hector," Uncle Gord said.

"Huh?"

"Hurricane Hector. Late last fall. You know, the biggest storm to hit Florida in two hundred years. The lawyers figure the storm moved the sand around. The same sand that was covering the pirate ship. Their guess is that the storm also spread the coins out from the ship."

Uncle Gord took a paper napkin. With a pencil from his pocket, he began to draw the different islands around Key Largo. He also drew some arrows going south to north.

"Here's the Gulf current," he said, pointing at the arrows. "You know how strong it is."

I did. All divers did. The giant current was caused by water heating in the hot tropics near the equator and flowing north, where the water cooled again.

"These lawyers got charts from weather scientists," Uncle Gord continued. "The charts showed the currents and the movement of Hurricane Hector. The charts also showed how strong the current was during the storm and how fast it moved. From those charts and from where the coins were found, they have tried to track the coins."

I became excited. "Because if they can track the coins, they can track them back to where they came from."

Uncle Gord grinned. "Now you know why I agreed to help the lawyers. They believe they have the spot of the sunken ship narrowed down. It's in an area twenty miles long and half a mile wide. Right where the Gulf current is the strongest."

His grin became a frown. "But twenty miles long and half a mile wide is still ten square miles. That's a lot of ocean bottom to explore. Especially for one boat only going out on weekends. We look around and mark off the area on our map so we don't go back to it again. We figure it might take a year or more to search all of it."

Thelma was coming toward us with our french fries. I waited until she was gone before I said anything.

"That's why you wanted people to think you were spearfishing," I said. "You don't want anyone else to look for it."

Uncle Gord dipped one of his fries into ketchup. "Exactly," he said. "Night is a great time to do it. We have good underwater lights and fewer people can see us. But from what you said, it's not much of a secret anymore. And that's bad news for two reasons."

"Why?"

"One, I have no idea how the secret got out. Maybe one of the three lawyers is trying a double cross."

"And the other reason?" I asked. Hungry as I was, I hadn't touched my fries yet.

"I don't know if you noticed," Uncle Gord said. "But the scuba tanks that you and Judd took out today? They're the tanks I usually use. I'm afraid someone wants *me* dead."

Chapter Eight

The next day I went to work as usual in the dive shop.

Uncle Gord's dive shop has four rooms. The sales floor has scuba diving gear: masks, flippers, wet suits, spearguns, tanks, books on the sport. Everything.

At one side is a doorway to another long and narrow room. This is the training room. It has a long table where up to twelve people can sit. At one end is a chalkboard. Uncle Gord uses this room when he gives dry land lessons on scuba diving.

There is also a back room. This has the workbench where we looked at the broken spring. It is where we fill the scuba diving tanks with air. It is where we do repairs.

The last room is Uncle Gord's office. It is tiny. Hardly bigger than his messy desk. He always keeps its door locked so customers don't wander in.

I spent most of the day talking to customers. We not only sell scuba diving stuff and train people, we also take people on diving trips. Uncle Gord has several people working for him, including me and Judd.

Since it was Friday, it was busier than it had been earlier in the week. A lot of divers come down to Key Largo for the weekend. They want tanks filled with air. They like to ask for advice on where to dive.

At six o'clock, I was the last one out of the shop. Uncle Gord was down at the dock, getting his boat ready for the night. I locked the store and walked to Thelma's diner for a burger and fries.

When I finished eating, I went to the cash register to pay.

"That's four dollars and fifty cents," she said.

"Sure." I reached for my wallet. I couldn't find it.

"Nuts," I said. "I left my money at the dive shop."

"No problem," Thelma said. "You can pay me tomorrow."

"Actually," I said, "I'll just run back and get my wallet. It won't take me long at all."

But it took a lot longer than I figured.

After I opened the front door, I saw that Uncle Gord's office door was open. But the light wasn't on inside.

Are we being robbed?

I wondered if I should call the police. I remembered that Uncle Gord wanted negative stuff kept secret. So I hid behind the counter instead. I waited to see who had broken into Uncle Gord's office.

It took five minutes for the person to step out of the office. It shouldn't have surprised me, but it did.

Judd Warner. And he had a pistol in his hand.

Chapter Nine

I crouched farther behind the front counter. I waited for him to walk past and held my breath. I hoped he couldn't hear how loud my heart was beating.

Judd stepped past the counter. He didn't look behind him. He didn't see me.

He was wearing black pants and a black T-shirt. As he walked toward the back room, he folded a piece of paper and stuck it in his pocket. He lifted his shirt and put his pistol into his belt. He dropped the shirt to cover the gun.

The front door! I had unlocked it and let

myself in quietly. But I hadn't locked it behind me. If he went out the front, he'd know someone else was in the dive shop!

I held my breath longer. I watched his shadow. It took a step toward the front, then turned away. He stepped into the back room. A few moments later, the door at the back opened and closed. I heard the turn of the key. Judd locked the door behind him.

I stood.

What should I do?

If I called in the police, what would I tell them? It didn't look like Judd had taken money. Instead, it seemed like the piece of paper had been important. The police would ask me what was missing, and I wouldn't be able to tell them. Plus, it would be Judd's word against mine.

I wanted to let Uncle Gord know about this. But I didn't know exactly where Uncle Gord was.

I stood longer. Flies buzzed against the front window. Other than that, the dive shop was very quiet.

I thought of Uncle Gord and his search for the sunken pirate ship. Was Judd in Uncle Gord's office because of that?

Of course! Judd had just started working here. Maybe he'd heard rumors about the treasure. Maybe he wanted to work for Uncle Gord so he could spy on him.

Spy!

I thought of something else. It was strange that Judd was wearing black jeans and a black T-shirt. Although it was early evening, it was still very hot. Why wear black in this heat? I had never seen Judd wear black before.

I grinned at how smart I was. If you were going to follow people at night, wouldn't you wear something dark?

It was Friday night. Judd knew that Uncle Gord would be going out in the dive boat tonight. Judd was probably going to follow him. Maybe even go on board the dive boat. There was plenty of room to hide on it.

There were two ways to find out if I was right.

One of the ways, I'd tell Uncle Gord. He and his three friends from Miami would watch for Judd. But if they stopped him, it would be easy for Judd to come up with an excuse for being near the dive boat. And if I was wrong about Judd, I'd look stupid.

The other way was to keep my mouth shut and follow Judd. If he really was up to something wrong, I'd know it by watching him. But I'd already waited in the dive shop too long to know where he had gone. How could I catch up to him?

I slapped my forehead. If Judd was going to spy on Uncle Gord tonight, there was only one place Judd would go. To the dive boat.

I ran to the front door, let myself out, and locked it.

It was almost 7:00. In a couple of hours, the sun would set. By 9:00, Uncle Gord and his friends would be on the dive boat, getting ready to leave. If Judd was following them, he'd be there too.

With a few hours left until darkness, I didn't need to run. I forced myself to walk as I headed to Uncle Gord's beach house. That's where I lived for the summer. I'd be able to find dark clothes for me too.

Then I would be ready to hunt the hunter.

Chapter Ten

I reached the docks at 8:00. I had on a dark summer jacket and a pair of dark track pants.

I stood still and looked around. The smell of saltwater filled the air. Pelicans stood on the dock posts. There were dozens of boats roped to one long dock. A lot of people were walking around. None of them were Judd or Uncle Gord or the lawyers from Miami.

Past the docks, the sun had almost set. The sky was orange, a postcard kind of sunset. In less than half an hour, most of the light would be gone.

I already knew where I would wait and watch. I carried a gym bag in one hand. I had a fishing pole in my other hand. I had a cap low over my eyes. I was going to sit at the end of the dock where I could keep an eye on Uncle Gord's dive boat, the *GypSea*.

It was the fourth boat down. The *GypSea* bobbed in the water as passing boats made wake.

I walked onto the dock. The *GypSea* was empty as I passed it. Fifty yards down, I reached the end of the dock. I sat and dropped my fishing line into the water. I held the fishing pole as if I were waiting for a fish to take bait. With a slight turn of my head, I kept an eye on the *GypSea*. Most of my face was hidden by my baseball cap.

Ten minutes later, Judd Warner walked onto the dock.

I ducked my head down even more. I didn't think he would give me a second look. He was probably too worried about getting on the *GypSea* to notice anybody fishing.

He hopped onto the *GypSea* as if he owned it. A second later, he had moved into the front of the boat. It was a big boat.

There were many places he could hide beneath the top deck. A few seconds later, he was out of sight.

My heart began to race. I had guessed right!

I waited a few more minutes. Once Judd was hidden, he wouldn't be able to see me get on the boat. As I waited, I went through my plan again. At this point, I could change my mind. I could wait for Uncle Gord and the lawyers to get to the boat. I could tell them about Judd. They could find him.

But then they would never know what he really meant to do. No, I told myself, the best way was to wait and see what Judd wanted. I told myself I would stick to my plan.

I stood and picked up the gym bag. I walked back down to the *GypSea*. Front to back it was sixty feet long. About twenty good-sized steps. It had a couple of cabins beneath the top deck. Judd was hidden there somewhere.

I stepped onto the boat as lightly as I could. I didn't want him to hear me.

The sun had dropped out of sight and the last rays of light made long shadows. I knew of a place where no one would see me during the day. It made it that much safer at night in the dark. I tiptoed to my hiding spot.

It was a wide locker where we stored wet suits that we rented to divers. I opened it and pushed myself among the wet suits. They smelled of saltwater.

There was just enough room inside for me to set my gym bag at my feet. I reached down and opened it.

First, I pulled out some string. I wanted to be able to hold the door open a few inches. If I had my fingers around the edge, someone might see them. So I tied one end of the string to the inside handle of the door. Now I could hold the string and not be seen.

After that, I reached into my gym bag again. I pulled out a speargun.

After all, Judd had a pistol. I needed to be armed too.

Chapter Eleven

At 9:00, it was completely dark. I heard voices as Uncle Gord and the lawyers stepped onto the boat. I heard clanking as they set down their scuba gear.

I didn't need to see them to know what they looked like. I had seen them a couple other times. All three looked like football players. They had short hair and square faces. I remembered seeing them and thinking lawyers like that would be good to scare judges.

I wasn't worried that they might open the locker I was hiding in. They wouldn't need any of the rental wet suits around me. They would be in their own wet suits. People who dive a lot don't like using rental wet suits. Why? It sounds gross, but there are no toilets underwater. Sometimes divers have to go so bad that they go in their wet suits. The water washes it away. Who wants to wear a rental wet suit and wonder if a stranger has done that in it?

The four of them moved around the boat. They didn't talk much. There were other sounds. The slapping of water against the boat. Laughter from parties on other boats tied to the dock. But on Uncle Gord's boat, not much except my own breathing against the wet suits.

I heard Uncle Gord's footsteps as he walked to the controls. He started the engine blowers. Boat engines are beneath the deck. Air doesn't move much there. If there are any gasoline fumes around the engines, the fumes could explode when the engines start. A blower fans the old air out to make it safe.

A few minutes later, Uncle Gord started both engines. They roared as he gave them gas. Once they were warm, he let them drop to a steady chug. He yelled out instructions to the three others to untie the ropes that held the boat.

Uncle Gord backed the boat away from the dock. He turned it and slowly pulled out of the marina. The boat rocked a little in the smooth water.

It took fifteen minutes to get to open water. Finally, he was able to give the engines full gas and take the boat to full speed. It bounced harder against the waves. The wet suits around me slapped me as the boat moved up and down.

Uncle Gord ran the engines hard for another twenty minutes. Then he shut them down and the boat slowed to a stop.

I heard clanking. Uncle Gord had hit the switch to drop the anchor. There was a small motor that unwound the anchor chain. The motor whined and the chain clanked as the anchor fell through the water. I counted the seconds. When the clanking stopped, I guessed we were in 80 feet of water.

Through the crack of the open door, I saw the beams of flashlights as they got their equipment ready. I wondered why Uncle Gord didn't turn on any lights to help them.

Then I noticed I didn't see any of the small boat lights. They were supposed to be on to let other boaters know where we were.

At first, that seemed strange. Uncle Gord always does things the safe way.

Then I figured it out. They were here to look for ten million dollars in pirate's gold. They had spent every weekend searching in secret. They didn't *want* anyone to know where they were. So why should this weekend be any different?

But it was.

Two people on board the boat didn't belong.

Chapter Twelve

I **nearly fell asleep.** I was standing in the locker. The wet suits pressing against me kept me from falling. Nothing had happened for at least an hour.

It was weird. None of them had even gone into the water yet. The boat just sat in darkness. They just sat without talking. If this was a search for treasure, why weren't they under water?

Were the four of them waiting for something? If so, what?

Judd Warner had been just as quiet as the

rest of us. Wherever he was hidden, he had decided to wait too.

I nodded off. My face hit a wet suit. It woke me.

I heard the faint sound of other engines.

A boat?

A few minutes later, I decided it was an airplane.

The sound grew closer.

Suddenly, the boat lights flashed on.

Then off.

Then on.

Then off. This time, the lights stayed off.

The airplane passed over us low and loud. It kept going.

I didn't get it. What had just happened?

Whatever it was, it meant action. The three lawyers from Miami were moving around the deck of the ship. One of them passed close to the locker. I heard his breathing through the crack of my open door.

Then splashing. One splash. Two splashes. Three. Three men had just entered the water.

I pushed the locker door open just enough to see the dark shadow of Uncle Gord. He stood at the edge of the boat. Far away I saw the faint lights of the shoreline.

What was happening?

I opened the door a little farther. Uncle Gord had his back to me. He was looking out over the water. I tried to look past him to see what he was waiting for.

I saw another dark shadow move quietly behind Uncle Gord.

Judd Warner! With his pistol out in front of him!

I quietly pushed open the locker door.

It was all in front of me. The deck of the boat. Judd Warner standing behind Uncle Gord. Uncle Gord looking into the water. And the black, black ocean beyond.

"Hands behind your back," Judd said in a low voice.

Uncle Gord started to move.

Judd stepped forward and pressed his pistol against Uncle Gord's back.

"Hands behind your back or I pull the trigger."

Slowly, Uncle Gord put his hands behind him.

Slowly, I stepped out of the locker. I had the loaded speargun in my hand.

"Good," Judd said to Uncle Gord. "It's a lot easier taking you before those three gorillas get back on the boat."

I heard a click. Judd Warner had just handcuffed Uncle Gord's wrists together.

I raised my speargun. The safety was still on, but Judd didn't have to know that. I was afraid I might trigger the spear by accident. The spear would not only go through Judd but also through Uncle Gord.

"Please drop your gun," I said in a shaky voice. "I've got a speargun, and I'll shoot if I have to."

Chapter Thirteen

You don't know what you're doing, Ian," Judd said. "You're making a mistake."

"I'm going to count to three. Then I shoot. One . . . two . . ."

Judd bent over and set the gun on the deck.

"Now unlock the handcuffs," I said.

"If you'll listen to me," Judd said. "You would know that—"

"One . . . two . . ."

Judd reached into his pocket. I watched carefully to make sure he wasn't going for a knife. A few seconds later, he unlocked Uncle Gord.

Uncle Gord turned around. "Ian?"

"I followed him," I explained. "I didn't want to tell you until I knew what was happening."

"I owe you," Uncle Gord said. "Keep him covered while I get the gun."

I held the speargun at Judd's chest. Judd kept still. I couldn't see his face in the dark. Just the outline of his body.

When Uncle Gord had the pistol in his hand, he handcuffed Judd Warner. Uncle Gord put the key in his pocket.

"We can relax now, Ian," Uncle Gord said, stepping away from Judd. "This guy won't be able to do anything to us."

"What's going on?" I asked. "This doesn't look like a treasure hunt."

"You're smart, Ian," Uncle Gord told me. "That's what I've always liked about you."

Uncle Gord was backing away from Judd as he spoke. He kept the pistol pointed at Judd as he moved beside me.

"This is weird," I said. "What is Judd doing here?"

"I'll tell you in a second," Uncle Gord said. "I really hate doing this." He turned to me, and in a single movement, pressed the pistol against my head. "First, I want you to throw the speargun overboard."

"Huh?"

"I know I'm your uncle. But I'm not going to let that stop me. Throw your speargun into the water behind you. I'm not joking. If you don't, I'll be forced to put a neat little hole into your head."

I was frozen with disbelief.

I heard the pistol click as Uncle Gord brought the hammer back.

I threw the speargun behind me. It splashed into the darkness a second later.

"See," Uncle Gord said. "You are smart. Now stand beside Judd where I can watch both of you."

This wasn't real, I told myself. It felt like I was walking through waist-deep glue as I moved beside Judd.

"Look behind you," Uncle Gord said. "That's your answer."

At first, I saw nothing but black. It hurt my eyes, I was looking so hard. Finally, I thought I saw something. For a moment, I wondered if it was my imagination. It seemed like a speck of light on the water.

A few seconds later, I knew my eyes were not playing tricks on me. The speck of light glowed brighter and brighter. It was heading right toward the boat.

Then, in a flash, I put it all together. The boat sitting in the dark for an hour. Waiting for an airplane to pass overhead. Lights flashing to let the airplane know the boat was there. Something in the water, marked by a glow light.

I didn't want to believe it, but it couldn't be anything else. Uncle Gord wasn't searching for treasure on his Friday and Saturday nights.

Instead, it could only be one thing.

Drugs.

Chapter Fourteen

I knew a little about drug running. A person can't live in Florida long without learning that drugs are big business. Florida had the wide-open ocean. It was the perfect place to move drugs into the rest of the United States. It's against the law, of course. But that doesn't stop a lot of people. Drugs are also big money.

My Uncle Gord. A drug dealer.

I wanted to kick myself for ever believing the three big guys were lawyers. They were built like football players. These were the kind of guys you wanted around if you were breaking the law. You wanted them around if you were working with dope dealers who didn't care if they murdered to make their money.

Thinking about it, I saw that Uncle Gord's plan was perfect. First, he told people they were spearfishing at night. It was easy to believe that's why they went out on weekends. After all, Uncle Gord ran a scuba diving business for a living.

Then to make sure people were really fooled, he probably started the rumors about a treasure hunt. It was like a lie behind a lie. Who would ever guess there was a third lie behind the second lie?

"You use this boat for pickups, don't you?" I said to Uncle Gord. "Business has been bad. You're making extra money by coming out here to pick up drugs dropped from an airplane. Those three guys went into the water to get them."

"You're almost right," Uncle Gord said. "We're anchored on the edge of the Gulf current. Whatever drops from the plane will pass close to this boat. And yes, the three men are out there to look for it and pick it up."

Splashing noises reached us. They were close to the boat now. I took a quick peek. The light bobbed in the water. I couldn't see much around it, except the heads and shoulders of the scuba divers.

"Boys," Uncle Gord called out to them. "Come in real easy. We've got company. Nothing for you to worry about, but I didn't want you surprised."

"The FBI clown?" one of the voices called up to the boat.

"Yup," Uncle Gord said.

"How do we know he isn't holding a gun to your head?" one of the other voices asked.

Uncle Gord stepped to the control panels of the boat. He flicked on a light. It showed him clearly. His gray hair. His bushy mustache. The gun in his hand. And a cold, cold stare in his eyes.

Uncle Gord snapped the light off again. "You saw enough to know I'm in charge?"

"We're coming aboard," came the answer.

There were more splashing sounds.

One man stepped onto the deck near us, dripping water from his wet suit. A second man. And a third. All big. Very big.

What surprised me was the fourth man. Much shorter than the other three. Where had he come from?

"What is going on?" the short man asked in an angry voice. He had a strong Spanish accent. "FBI? This was not part of our agreement."

Chapter Fifteen

If it makes you feel better, Ian," Uncle Gord said, "I'm not into drugs."

I wasn't sure anything could make me feel better. Judd was an FBI agent, and I'd put him into this trouble. My uncle was pointing a gun at me. And three big guys were behind him to help.

"Enough talk," one of the big guys said.

"What difference does it make?" Uncle Gord asked. "I've got the gun. They're not going anywhere. And this is our last run anyway."

To me, Uncle Gord said. "Cubans. That's

what we do. Help Cubans make it into the United States. We help them become citizens. We help them leave behind a terrible life."

"Don't buy that," Judd Warner said. He hadn't spoken in a while. Coming out of the darkness beside me, his voice surprised me.

"Oh, really," Uncle Gord told Judd. "If you're so smart, you tell Ian."

"Not many Cubans can afford your uncle," Judd said to me. "The man standing in front of us is a wanted criminal. He got his money by dealing drugs in Cuba."

"Shoot this man!" the short Cuban shouted.

"Not yet," Uncle Gord said. "I want to hear more."

Judd didn't say anything.

Uncle Gord pointed his gun at my chest. "Tell us what you know, Mr. FBI, or the kid dies."

"I know it was me you tried to kill with the broken valve on the scuba tank," Judd said.

"Yes," Uncle Gord said. "We've been onto you for a least a week. You asked a few too many questions. We did want you dead before tonight, but it had to look like an accident."

"You wrecked the tank?" I said to Uncle Gord. "But, but . . ."

"Sorry," he said. It didn't sound like he meant it. "That's the way it goes."

Sorry? All he said was sorry? This was my uncle. My mother's brother. The guy I had been visiting every summer since I was fourteen.

"Keep going," Uncle Gord said to Judd. "What else do you know?"

The boat bobbed gently in the waves. A nice warm breeze crossed my face. Just a regular Florida night. It seemed unreal to be watching my uncle with a gun in his hand.

"It's simple," Judd said. "You've got a pilot in a seaplane who picks them up from a rowboat off Cuba's shore. You know that airplanes are watched on radar. It's too risky to bring people into Florida that way. So they drop them into the water, and you pick them up. You hide them on the boat and bring them in. You have fake passports ready for them and send them on their way."

"One hundred thousand dollars," Uncle Gord told me. "Divide it four ways. That's twenty-five grand for each of us every Friday and Saturday night."

Uncle Gord shook his head sadly. "Yes, Ian, it was a great way to make money. Too bad it ends tonight. This guy works for the FBI. I'm sure he's been filing reports. Even after he's dead, we'll have trouble. So today we decided this run is our last."

After he's dead? My uncle was going to kill a man?

"And by the way, Ian," Uncle Gord said. "We'll have to kill you too."

Chapter Sixteen

After we drop the Cuban off, we're disappearing to the Bahamas for a while," Uncle Gord said to the men behind him. "We might as well put weights on these two and let them go off the wall. That way, no one will ever find their bodies."

I felt my knees go weak.

Off the wall.

Uncle Gord was talking about the continental shelf. For about the first three miles from shore, the ocean didn't get much deeper than 150 feet. The land beneath the water was like a shelf.

But three miles out, the land just dropped away. It was like stepping off the edge of a table. Divers called it going off the wall. The ocean went from 150 feet deep to 10,000 feet. Nearly two miles straight down into deep, deep blackness.

"Good idea," one of the men said. "No bodies, no more trouble."

Uncle Gord handed the pistol to the closest man. "Cover me," Gord said. "I'm going to handcuff them together. If one of them even blinks, shoot."

Uncle Gord dug the handcuff key out of his pocket. He unsnapped the cuffs. Then he cuffed Judd's left hand to my right hand.

"Keep covering them," Uncle Gord said. "One of you get behind the wheel. Take the boat in so we can drop off the Cuban. While we're moving, I'm going to wire the spare anchor to the handcuffs."

As the boat moved toward shore, Uncle Gord wired a length of anchor chain to the middle of the handcuffs. The other end of the chain had the heavy anchor.

I kept hoping that Judd would do something to save us. I mean, he was an FBI undercover agent. Didn't he have some kind of training?

But the whole time, there was a pistol pointed at us. Judd didn't try anything.

Before we reached Key Largo, Uncle Gord brought out some tape.

"How could you do this?" I said.

Uncle Gord shrugged. "Twice a week since the beginning of May. Do your math. I'm nearly a million dollars richer. I'm not going to jail, not when I'm that rich. And I can't trust you to keep your mouth shut."

"But I'm your nephew."

"Hey," he said. "If you're going to kill someone, how much worse can it be that they're related?"

He taped our mouths so Judd and I couldn't yell for help when we got to Key Largo.

The boat reached the docks. They kept us out of sight. They dropped the Cuban off. Then they headed back out in the darkness.

Toward the deep, deep water. Where they were going to drop us off the wall.

Chapter Seventeen

I guess the worst way to die is to see it coming ahead of time. If you have a car accident or something like that, you don't have time to worry.

Instead, I was on a boat going 30 knots. I knew that in a couple of miles, I would be thrown overboard. That was not enough time left. It was way too much time left.

I thought of everything nice I would miss. Orange sunsets. The feel of sand on my bare feet, of sun on my skin.

I thought of my parents. Sometimes we fought, but I loved them. And I knew they always tried to do what was best for me. I wished I could let them know I loved them. I wished I'd said it more times when I was around them.

I thought of Sunday school when I was a kid. I thought I should have listened better. I hoped heaven was waiting.

And I cried. Not sobbing crying, like a little baby. But tears of sadness that the wind pushed across my face. This was sad. And I was scared.

Chapter Eighteen

It took all four of them. Uncle Gord and the three big ugly guys.

One of them lifted me. One of them lifted Judd. And two of them lifted the anchor that was hooked between our handcuffs.

I couldn't yell at them. My mouth was still taped shut.

I didn't kick at them. I had given up. What chance did I have? It was two miles straight down in the black water. The anchor was so heavy that it took two guys to lift. It was going to pull me and Judd down like a piano falling through air.

Judd didn't fight either.

"We'll toss them on the count of three," Uncle Gord said. Like we were just a couple sacks of potatoes.

"One . . ."

They swung once. They hadn't even slowed the boat.

"Two . . ."

A bigger swing.

"Three!"

They let go on the third upswing. We cleared the edge of the boat and dropped through the air.

I drew one final breath.

Then . . .

Splash. Just one sound. Judd and I and the anchor hit the water all at the same time.

The water was cold. We dropped in total black silence.

Chapter Nineteen

We fell, fell, fell. We fell so fast that the water peeled my shirt and pant legs upward.

And still we fell into the deep black.

My lungs began to hurt. Any second I wouldn't be able to help myself. I would suck for air. All I would get was water. I would be dead long before we hit the ocean floor two miles down.

Then, suddenly, the water stopped tugging at me.

I was free!

Both my arms could move!

71

My lungs were screaming for air. I bit down hard and kicked my legs.

Up, up, I told myself, kick up!

I fought against the water. I had to get to the surface. All I could think of was reaching air.

I kicked. But the harder I kicked, the more I needed air.

I kicked. I felt myself growing weaker, but still I kicked.

And I reached cool air. The black of water was now the black of night. With stars above. I tried to gasp for air, but my mouth was taped. I got a little air through my nostrils, but I needed more. I ripped the tape from my mouth and pulled in lungful after lungful of air.

The noise of the *GypSea* grew fainter and fainter as it left me behind.

I took in more air. It was great to be alive.

It hit me. *I was alive*. What had happened? Where was Judd?

There was a splash beside me.

"Judd?" I called out.

I heard him gasping. Then he answered.

"Over here." His voice croaked just like mine.

We kept splashing until we were side by side. We dog paddled to keep our heads above the water.

"I can't believe this," I said. "How did you do that?"

He laughed. "It's the first thing they taught us in the FBI. No matter what, always keep two handcuff keys. I keep the spare one in my sock."

He stopped to cough out water. "I didn't dare reach for it until we were in the water. I prayed I wouldn't drop it. I had to unlock your side first. If I didn't, you'd still be dropping and I'd have no way to catch you. . . ."

"Um, thanks," I said.

"Don't thank me yet," he said. "We're miles from shore. And I'm not a good swimmer. And I'm scared of sharks."

"Let me show you something," I said. "You got us out of the cuffs. I'll get you to land."

Chapter Twenty

And I did get us there. From diving, I knew a few things that Judd didn't.

Sharks look for quick, hard movements. It makes them think of scared or hurt fish. Scared or hurt fish make them think of food.

Judd and I did our best to float without moving much. If sharks passed below us, they'd see something that looked like a log. And since we weren't cut, there was no blood for them to smell.

We did the "dead man's float." To do it, all you do is take a big breath. It fills your lungs with air and helps you float. When you breathe out, you paddle a bit to keep your head above the water. Then breathe in and put your face back in the water.

We floated for ten hours.

We watched the sun rise.

We watched land get closer as the Gulf current moved us in the ocean.

And with shouts of joy, we finally saw a boat on the water. The people on it didn't see us at first. We waved our arms and shouted. Still, they didn't see us. Finally, a little boy on the boat pointed toward us. His parents bent over as they listened to him. They stood up and looked in our direction. They waved at us and brought the boat over to rescue us.

We were back on shore by noon.

And, because we had heard Uncle Gord talk about going to the Bahamas, we knew where to send the FBI. Uncle Gord thought Judd and I were long dead. He never expected anyone to look for him. He was arrested three days later, on the beach. He thought he would be rich and able to hang out in the sun for the rest of his life.

Two months later, Uncle Gord and I stared at each other across the floor of a

Miami courthouse. The trial lasted one week. I spent one morning of that week on the witness stand. I told the judge and jury what had happened.

I still remember the last afternoon of the trial. It was right after the judge had sentenced Uncle Gord to thirty years in prison. The guard was walking him past me to take him to jail. Uncle Gord stopped to talk.

The sunlight came in through the window and put a shadow on his face. He looked years older.

"Ian," he said. "I don't get it. I listened to you tell the jury your story. You didn't even seem angry. I thought you would really hate me."

"Uncle Gord," I said. "I'm not going to hate you. I've decided I'm not going to give you that kind of power."

"Huh?"

"It would take energy to hate you. And there would be nothing to do about that hate except hate you more. Why should I make you such a big part of my life? I'm going to move on. I've got better things to do."

I shrugged. "Besides, if someone's tried to

kill you, how much worse can it be that he's a relative?"

And Now, a Word from the Author . . .

Dear Reader:

Forgiveness. It's one of the greatest messages that Jesus Christ preached when he walked through the land of Galilee.

He taught that when we are hurt, we are supposed to forgive others for their sake. Once we forgive them—especially if they are truly sorry—then they can move on. In other words, the one who has been wronged must forgive the wrongdoer in order to help that person.

Forgiveness, then, is a wonderful gift offered by the person who was hurt. It is an even greater gift when the wrongdoer has not offered an apology or asked for forgiveness.

And forgiveness truly is a great gift. If you have ever hurt someone—by accident or not—you know what it feels like when that person offers to forgive your mistake. That is why Jesus Christ is the greatest gift of all. God has offered through Him to forgive all our mistakes!

I believe, however, there is more to it than that, more to it than a gift from the wronged to the wrongdoer. It is something we might not stop to think about very often.

In His wisdom, Jesus Christ knew that the act of forgiving would also heal the forgiver.

After all, if you chose not to forgive someone, you hold on to the hurt. If you hold on to that hurt, it will only make you miserable again and again and again—long after the action itself happened. Yet if you can release that hurt, it will only hurt you once. (Think of a bumblebee. After it stings you, do you want to cup it in your hand so it can keep stinging you?)

Forgiveness, then, is more than a gift to

the wrongdoer. It is also the act of letting go of the hurt. It is a gift to yourself.

Ian Hill, at the end of *Off the Wall*, shows that wisdom. Ian doesn't want to waste his life thinking about the terrible thing his uncle did. Instead, Ian has decided not to keep the hatred. As Ian says, he has better things to do. Why should a black hatred keep him from enjoying all the good things that life has to offer?

No matter what your situation, along with a list of things that have hurt you, you can also make a long, long list of good things in your life. Knowing that, you have a choice. You can put your heart in the sunshine that comes with keeping your thoughts on good things. Or you can bury your heart in the black cave of remembering a much smaller list of bad things.

I think the choice is easy.

From your friend,

Sigmund Brouwer

Read and collect all of
Sigmund Brouwer's

Turn the page for an exciting preview of

SKYDIVING

...to the Extreme:

'Chute Roll

Jeff Nichols works at a local flight school—just to pay for his skydiving. Then he hears of a plan to put his biggest rival into a 'chute roll, which no skydiver has ever survived. But trying to stop it might put Jeff in an airplane at 10,000 feet—without his parachute.

I held my breath. Although I have jumped more than 200 times, pulling the rip cord is the one thing that makes me nervous. For a few seconds, I always wonder if my 'chute will open. In my nightmares, I'm falling toward the ground. In my nightmares, I have wo or three minutes to watch it rush toward me. In my nightmares, I have all that time to wonder what it will feel like to smash into the ground.

I held my breath and counted the seconds. One, two, three . . .

Bang!

My shoulder straps jerked me as the 'chute opened wide. It slowed my fall from a 120 miles per hour to 10 miles per hour. It slowed me so quickly that it seemed to yank me upward, like a giant hand pulling me from above.

I started to breathe again. Now all I had to do was guide myself toward the target as I floated downward.

I looked over my shoulder to see where Sabella was. I spotted her about a minute behind me. She was a dark shape against the pale blue sky.

I checked the ground.

I checked Sabella.

I checked the ground again.

I checked Sabella. And nearly screamed.

Her 'chute had tangled!

The strings of the parachute were all wound together, and it could not fill with air.

She tumbled toward me. Because I was floating and she was in free fall, she gained on me like a rock.

I saw her pull the breakaway cord and release her main 'chute. She yanked at her second rip cord to open her reserve parachute.

Nothing happened. No 'chute opened behind her.

I couldn't hear her scream, but her mouth was wide open in terror.

A second later, she flashed past me on her way toward death.

There was only one thing to do. I had to cut myself loose from my parachute.

I arched my back. If you don't do a breakaway right, you get thrown into a spin. Once I was level, I pulled on the breakaway handle.

It took less than a second to lose my main 'chute.

I fell toward the ground. I dropped my head and pointed my arms straight down into a dive position.

Sabella was falling belly first. She had her arms and legs wide to slow herself as much as possible. You've got a one in a million chance to survive a free fall, but she was trying.

In my dive, I started to gain on her. By cutting through the air in a dive, you can go from 120 miles per hour up to 200 miles per hour.

She was a little ahead and to the left. I kicked a leg out to change my direction. I aimed straight at her.

The wind screamed against my face and goggles.

Twenty seconds later, I had cut the distance in half. Ten seconds later, I had cut it in half again.

But the ground was getting closer and closer. I could see the cross-like shadows of cactus trees. If I didn't reach Sabella soon . . .

Five, four, three, two . . .

Her dark hair was flapping from beneath her helmet like a blanket. It almost whipped in my face as I reached her. I had to time it just right. I flung out my hand and grabbed her ankle.

She screamed.

"Don't panic," I shouted.

With both hands, I pulled myself up her

body. The rushing wind tried to tear us apart. But I held on.

The ground was closer and closer still.

Finally, I yanked the second rip cord on my parachute. It was for my backup 'chute. I prayed it would open. . . .

As I waited those awful few seconds, I wrapped my arms around Sabella. I hugged her tight against my chest. I needed to be holding her with all my strength.

My 'chute flopped open and yanked at us.

I held tight. We were maybe a thousand feet off the ground and still traveling fast. Would there be enough time for the single parachute to slow down the weight of two people?